T. REX AND THE MOTHER'S DAY HUG

by Lois G. Grambling
illustrated by Jack E. Davis

KATHERINE TEGEN BOOKS
An Imprint of HarperCollins*Publishers*

Also by Lois G. Grambling and Jack E. Davis

T. Rex and the Mother's Day Hug

Text copyright © 2008 by Lois G. Grambling Illustrations copyright © 2008 by Jack E. Davis
Manufactured in China. All rights reserved.

For information address HarperCollins Children's Books, a division of
HarperCollins Publishers, 1350 Avenue of the Americas, New York, NY 10019.
www.harpercollinschildrens.com

Library of Congress Cataloging-in-Publication Data is available.
ISBN-10: 0-06-053126-6 (trade bdg.) — ISBN-13: 978-0-06-053126-3 (trade bdg.)
ISBN-10: 0-06-053127-4 (lib. bdg.) — ISBN-13: 978-0-06-053127-0 (lib. bdg.)

Typography by Sarah Hoy
1   2   3   4   5   6   7   8   9   10
❖
First Edition

To my children and grandchildren, who make
Mother's Day special for me by remembering
—L.G.G.

For my mother, who wrestled six little dinosaurs
through childhood with wonderful humor,
kindness, and love
—J.E.D.

T. Rex's doorbell rang. It was his friends Diplodocus, Stegosaurus, and Iguanodon. Each had a package.

"Mother's Day gifts?" T. Rex asked.

"You bet!" Diplodocus said.

"Are you **DOING** something for your mother again this year? Instead of **GETTING** her something?" Stegosaurus asked.

T. Rex nodded.

"What are you **DOING?**" Iguanodon asked.

"I haven't decided," T. Rex said.

"Better decide soon. Mother's Day is tomorrow," Diplodocus said.

"Call if you need any help," Stegosaurus said.

"I will," T. Rex said. "Thanks."

The next morning T. Rex rushed downstairs to see his mother.

"HAPPY MOTHER'S DAY, MAMA!" he said. "I want to DO something for you today. Something that will make you happy."

Mama Rex smiled. "A Mother's Day hug would make me happy, dear," she said.

"I want to DO more, Mama," T. Rex said. "MORE! Maybe I can go to Dinosaur Swamp and pick some ferns. And decorate the living room for you today."

But then T. Rex remembered. . . . He and his friends had done this before. And that had not made Mama happy.

Mama remembered too. (How could she forget?) The living room had turned into a rain forest! Muddy footprints and murky puddles were everywhere.

WHAT A MESS!

Mama Rex's brow folded into rows of wrinkles.
"A Mother's Day hug would make me happy,
dear!" she said.

"I want to DO more, Mama," T. Rex said.
"MORE! Maybe I can wallpaper the dining room
for you today. And make the dining room brighter."

But then T. Rex remembered. . . . He and his friends had done this before. And that had not made Mama happy.

Mama remembered too. (How could she forget?) T. Rex and his friends had papered over the windows. And over Great Aunt Bertha. The dining room was dark now. And Great Aunt Bertha was just a bulge on one wall.

WHAT A MESS!

Mama Rex's brow folded into big rows of wrinkles.

"A Mother's Day hug would make me very happy, dear!" she said.

"But I want to do **MORE!**" said T. Rex. What could he DO for Mama today?

He looked out the window. And saw Mama's car.

T. Rex hurried out the door. "I'll see you later, Mama!" he said.

Mama Rex went to the kitchen. Made
herself a cup of tea.
Sat down.

Waited.

AND WORRIED.

T. Rex called Diplodocus, Stegosaurus, and Iguanodon. They came right over. And the four friends started DOING things to Mama's car.

Diplodocus painted a frowning T. Rex on the grille.

Stegosaurus painted racing stripes on both sides.

Iguanodon hammered a shiny ornament onto the hood.

T. Rex painted and pasted ferns here and there and everywhere.

And when there was absolutely no more they could
DO, T. Rex added a sign on the side that read:

MAMA'S REX MOBILE

T. Rex stepped back and admired Mama's Rex Mobile.
Diplodocus, Stegosaurus, and Iguanodon stepped
back—and decided to leave before Mama Rex saw it!

T. Rex called to his mama. "Come out now, Mama."
Mama Rex hurried out. And gasped! "That's . . .
that's my car?" she asked. (Hoping it wasn't!)
T. Rex grinned. "Now you won't have trouble finding
your car when you park at the mall, Mama," he said.
Mama's brow folded into bigger rows of wrinkles.
"I'm sure I won't, dear!" she said.

"HAPPY MOTHER'S DAY, MAMA,"
T. Rex said, giving his mama a very big hug!

Suddenly all of Mama's rows of wrinkles disappeared. And a very big smile spread across her face.

"That Mother's Day hug made me very happy, dear," she said. **"THAT'S** what I wanted most for Mother's Day!"

"I love you **SOOO** much, Mama," T. Rex said.
"I know, dear," Mama Rex said. "I love you **SOOO** much too."
Even though Mama Rex loved T. Rex **SOOO** much, she was **SOOO** happy Mother's Day came only once a year.

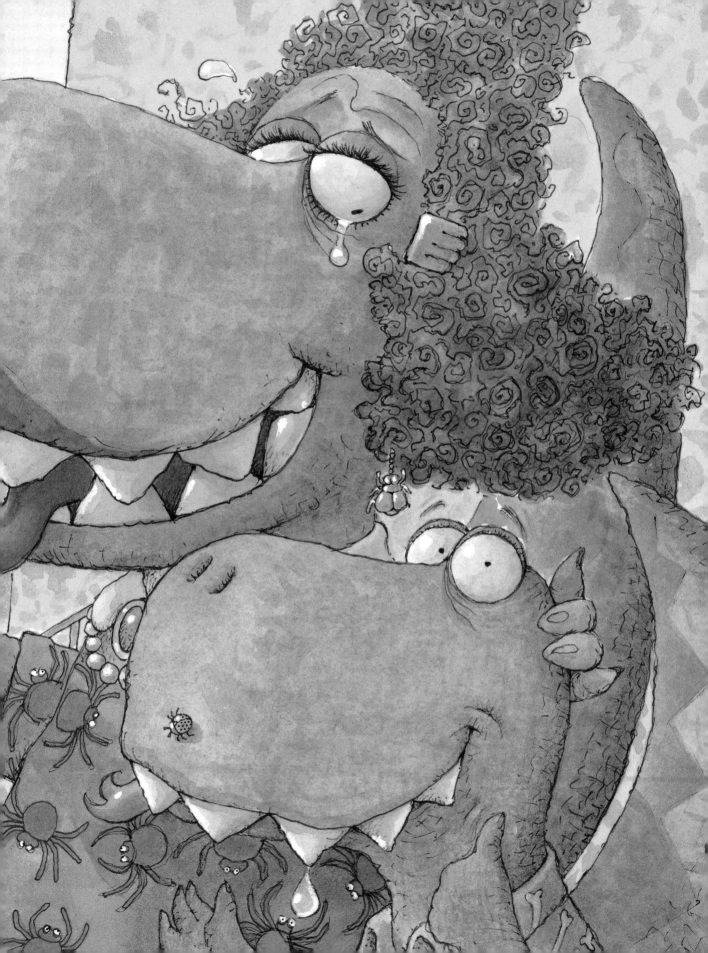